THE NUT MAP

SUSANNA GRETZ

THE NUT MAP

SUSANNA GRETZ

MAMMOTH

First published in Great Britain 1996
by W H Books Ltd and Mammoth, imprints of Reed International Books Ltd
Michelin House, 81 Fulham Road, London SW3 6RB
and Auckland, Melbourne, Singapore and Toronto
10 9 8 7
Text and illustrations copyright © Susanna Gretz 1996
The author has asserted her moral rights
Paperback ISBN 0 7497 2347 5
Hardback ISBN 0 434 97458 7
A CIP catalogue record for this title
is available from the British Library
Produced by Mandarin Offset Ltd
Printed at Oriental Press, Dubai, U.A.E.

Vera has never seen winter before.

'Never seen winter before – think of that,'

says Jack. He's older and larger than Vera.

'When can we hide some nuts?' asks Vera.

'Not yet, silly,' says Jack.

The leaves begin to fall.

'Is it winter now?' asks Vera.

'Of course not, it's autumn,' says Jack.

'Is it time to hide nuts?' asks Vera.

'Not yet, silly!' says Jack.

Have another apple!

The days grow colder. It's nearly winter.

'Now is it time to hide nuts?' asks Vera.

'Yes,' says Jack, 'but the trick is to

remember where you hid them.'

'Then you dig them up again,' explains
Jack, 'when there's no fresh food left.'
Vera looks worried. 'We'll never find them,'
she says. 'Unless we make a nut map!'
Jack thinks this is ridiculous.

'Whenever we want to find our nuts

we can check the map,' continues Vera.

'I can't be bothered,' says Jack.

'Can you always find yours?' asks Vera.

'Of course,' says Jack.

Vera finds some felt-tip pens and a large piece of paper. In one corner of the paper she draws her nest high up in the oak tree. When she looks down she can see a path, a frog pond, a tree stump and lots more.

Vera draws them all on her map.

Then she rolls up the map

and tucks it under her arm.

Vera hides a nut.

Then she marks her map.

Jack is hiding nuts, too.

The days go by.

Each time Vera hides more nuts

she draws an ✗ on the map.

One day Vera sees a blackbird
watching them.

'Why is he watching us?' asks Vera.

'Because he...' But Jack isn't looking

where he is going.

He trips over something in the leaves.

It's Dickie Shuffle, the hedgehog.

'I was building my winter nest here,'

snaps Dickie.

'Sorry,' says Jack.

15

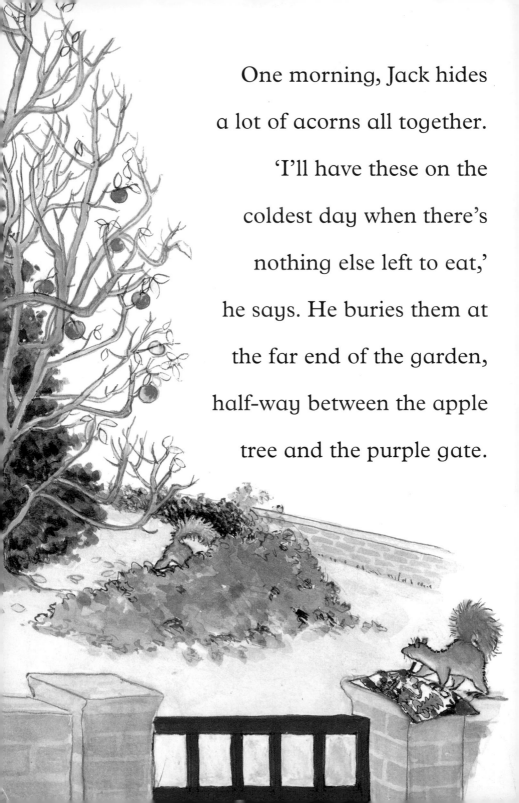

One morning, Jack hides
a lot of acorns all together.
'I'll have these on the
coldest day when there's
nothing else left to eat,'
he says. He buries them at
the far end of the garden,
half-way between the apple
tree and the purple gate.

At last the weather turns icy cold. The two squirrels have eaten the last blackberry, the last rosehip and the last apple.

'Now we must find those nuts,' says Jack.

'I'll get my map,' says Vera.

Not that silly map again!

It's not silly.

garden wall ↗

frog
pond ↑

leaves

tree stump ↙

x

x

x

x

x

Nut Map

path →

← nest

Jack and Vera start hunting.

'Now where did I bury

those hazel nuts?'

Vera checks her map.

'Between the pine tree

and the old shed...

got them!'

Vera gobbles them up.

The next day Vera fancies some acorns.

'Now where did I bury them?

Let's check the map.

In the corner by the garden wall,

under the holly bush...found them!'

'And where are those beech nuts?

Near the path, behind the tree stump...'

'I can *smell* the nuts I buried,' says Jack.

'I don't need a map.'

'Well I do!' says Vera.

Each day Vera finds just

enough nuts to keep herself going.

Then she rolls up her map

and heads for home.

One morning at the coldest end of winter,

everything looks different outside.

'What's that?' asks Vera.

'Snow, of course,' says Jack.

'It's so cold,' moans Vera,

'and I've eaten nearly all my nuts.'

But Jack isn't worried.

'I've got a huge pile of acorns,' he says,

'all buried in a special hidey-hole.'

'I remember that hidey-hole,'

says Vera. 'Let's look at the map.'

But Jack won't listen.

'Not that silly map again,' he says.

Jack marches off into the snow.

But where is Jack's hidey-hole?

He can't see it anywhere.

He sniffs and sniffs.

He can't smell it either.

Where is it?

He decides to ask the blackbird.

'Have you seen my acorns?'

No. I don't even **like** acorns.

Then he asks a rabbit and a mouse:

'Have you seen my acorns?'

No one knows where the acorns are

hidden, so Jack just keeps hunting.

'Look out!' says a voice from the leaves.

It's Dickie Shuffle.

'I'm sleeping,' mumbles Dickie.

'Sorry,' says Jack.

'Where are my acorns?' asks Jack.

'They were so beautiful...

and so delicious.'

Back home, Vera is hungry too.

'What's taking Jack so long?'

she wonders.

Then she hears him calling.

VERA...

VE-RA!

VE-RA!

32

She bounds off through the trees.

'Haven't you found those acorns yet?'

asks Vera.

'No,' says Jack in a very low voice,

'but – er – did you by any chance – er –

draw my hidey-hole on your map?'

Vera just stares at him.

'Oh, please, let's look at your map!'

begs Jack.

Vera unrolls the map.

They look at it very carefully.

'There!' cries Jack. 'Look at the ✗ !

That's where I hid my acorns...

...at the far end of the garden,

half-way between the apple tree

and the purple gate.'

'But that's right here,' says Dickie.

'YOU'RE RIGHT!' yell Jack and Vera.

Sure enough, the hidey-hole is

right under Dickie's nest, and

it is full of acorns.

'Look what you've done! You've ruined my nest!' shouts Dickie.

Vera and Jack want to say sorry, but their mouths are too full of acorns.

'It's all the fault of that stupid map,'

grumbles Dickie.

'It isn't stupid,' says Vera.

'If Vera hadn't made a map,' says Jack,

'we wouldn't have found the acorns.'

Jack thinks for a minute.

'If Dickie hadn't built his nest on top of my acorns,' he says, 'I would have smelled where they were, wouldn't I, Dickie?'

But Dickie has gone back to sleep.

'I would have,' says Jack.

'Rubbish!' says Vera.

Then she leaps up the apple tree...

and chases Jack all the way home.